D1430994

# Thief of Hearts

Adaptation by Karen Barss
Based on a TV series teleplay written by
Susan Kim and Ken Scarborough
**Based on the characters created by Susan Meddaugh**

HOUGHTON MIFFLIN HARCOURT
Boston • New York • 2011

Green Light Readers and its logo are trademarks of Houghton Mifflin Harcourt Publishing Company.

For information about permission to reproduce selections from this book, write to Permissions, Houghton Mifflin Harcourt Publishing Company, 215 Park Avenue South, New York, New York 10003.

Library of Congress Cataloging-in-Publication Data is on file.
ISBN 978-0-547-37162-7 pb
ISBN 978-0-547-39349-0 hc

Design by Rachel Newborn and Bill Smith Group

www.hmhbooks.com
www.marthathetalkingdog.com

Manufactured in China / LEO 10 9 8 7 6 5 4 3 2 1
4500246141

Everybody enjoys getting valentine cards. Martha does too!

Read this one!

"Let's make cards for each other,"
says Carolina.
Everyone likes that idea.

Everyone but Skits.
He wants to play in the snow!

Carolina is making her cards in the kitchen. "No peeking," she tells Skits.

T.D. draws in the living room.
"This card is for you, Martha!" says T.D.

Helen uses fabric to make her cards.
But Truman has a problem.

"I can't do this!" he says.

Me neither.
No thumbs.

"I'm not good at crafts,"
says Truman.
"Don't worry," says Helen. "Take a break."

They all have to take a break.
Carolina cannot find her glitter pen.
T.D. and Skits help her look for it.

Then T.D. says, "My notebook is missing."
Martha helps him look.
And Helen says, "Someone took my fabric!"

"Who took our supplies?" asks T.D.
"It's a mystery," Martha says.

Does Skits know who took the art supplies?
"Skits has something to show us," Martha says.

"Skits wants us to throw snowballs," says Martha. "Maybe later," she tells Skits.

Inside, the friends argue about
the missing things.

"I think I know who did it,"
Martha says.

She walks into the living room.

"Look under that sofa pillow," says Martha. Truman uncovers the missing supplies!

"But who did it?" Helen asks.
"Someone who always hides things there," says Martha.

"It's okay, Skits," Helen says.
"Were you feeling left out?"

"Let's throw snowballs to Skits!" says T.D.
"Cards can wait."
Truman likes this idea. They all do.

Now Skits is happy.
And everyone is having fun. Together.